FIRST FLIGHT®

*FIRST FLIGHT® is an exciting new series
of beginning readers.
The series presents titles which include songs,
poems, adventures, mysteries, and humour
by established authors and illustrators.
FIRST FLIGHT® makes the introduction to reading fun
and satisfying for the young reader.*

*FIRST FLIGHT® is available in 4 levels
to correspond to reading development.*

Level 1 – Preschool - Grade 1
Large type, repetition of simple concepts that are perfect for reading aloud, easy vocabulary and endearing characters in short simple stories for the earliest reader.

Level 2 – Grade 1 - Grade 3
Longer sentences, higher level of vocabulary, repetition, and high-interest stories for the progressing reader.

Level 3 – Grade 2 - Grade 4
Simple stories with more involved plots and a simple chapter format for the newly independent reader.

Level 4 – Grade 3 - up (First Flight Chapter Books)
More challenging level, minimal illustrations for the independent reader.

First four books in the First Flight® series

Level 1 • Jingle Bells *written and illustrated by* Maryann Kovalski

Level 2 • Fishes in the Ocean *written by* Maggee Spicer *and* Richard Thompson, *illustrated by* Barbara Hartmann

Level 3 • Andrew's Magnificent Mountain of Mittens
written by Deanne Lee Bingham, *illustrated by* Kim LaFave

Level 4 • The Money Boot *written by* Ginny Russell, *illustrated by* John Mardon

A First Flight® Level Three Reader

Andrew's Magnificent Mountain of Mittens

By
Deanne Lee Bingham

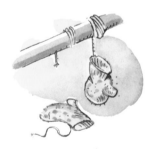

Illustrated
by Kim LaFave

Fitzhenry and Whiteside • Toronto

FIRST FLIGHT® is a registered trademark of Fitzhenry and Whiteside

First published in the United States in 1999.

Fitzhenry & Whiteside acknowledges with thanks the support of the
Government of Canada through its Book Publishing Industry Development
Program in the publication of this title.

Design by Wycliffe Smith Design

Printed in Canada.

10 9 8 7 6 5 4 3 2 1

Canadian Cataloguing in Publication Data

Bingham, Deanne Lee, 1963-
Andrew's magnificent mountain of mittens

(A first flight level 3 reader)
ISBN 1-55041-397-X (bound)
ISBN 1-55041-389-9 (pbk.)

I. LaFave, Kim. II. Title. III. Series.

PS8553.I64A76 1998   jC813'.54   C98-931738-2
PZ7 B56An 1998

With love,
for my sister Colleen Kleven
and my brother David Bingham.

Deanne

For Cameron,
my son, who inspired me
to create Andrew.

Kim

Andrew's Magnificent Mountain of Mittens

Chapter One

Every day Andrew would get
ready for school.

He'd zip up his coat,
slip on his boots,
tie on his scarf,
pop on his hat
and pull on his mittens.

But every night when he came home,
his mittens would be gone.

By late December Andrew
had lost every pair of mittens
he owned.

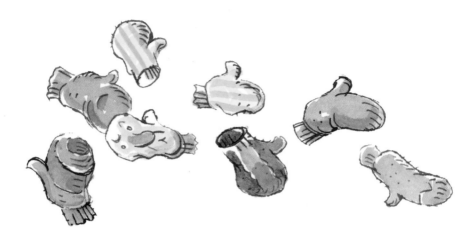

He'd lost a blue pair,
a yellow pair, a black pair,
an orange pair, a red pair,
a gray pair, a white pair,
a monster-face pair,
and even the pair
that his aunt had made
for him.

Andrew's parents
told Grandma the problem.

Grandma had an idea.

For Christmas, she knit Andrew
a pair of green mittens
attached with a string.

Andrew's mom and dad
were very relieved.

So was Andrew.

Chapter Two

The first day of school
after Christmas vacation,
Andrew went in early.
He climbed the jungle gym,
tangled his mittens and string
in the monkey bars,
had to be cut free,
and then lost his mittens—
all before the morning bell.

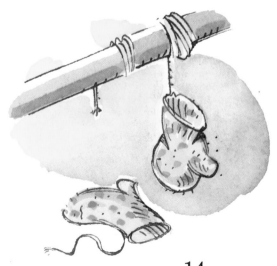

Andrew worried all morning.
What would he tell his family?
What should he do?

He took a piece of paper
and different-colored crayons
and began to draw.

When it was his turn
for Show and Tell,
he was ready.

Andrew held up his picture.
At the top it read

LOST By OWNER

and it was filled with drawings
of different-colored mittens —
all of the mittens that Andrew
had lost.

He had even drawn a picture
of the green ones his grandma
made, with little arrows
pointing to the strings.

His teacher thought that
this was a very good idea,
and so did all of his friends.

Ben suggested that Andrew
make more posters and put
them up around the school.
Ekoni said she would help,
and Derek offered to
hang the posters up.

By the end of the school day,
all of Andrew's classmates
were helping.

They hung posters in the hallway,
they taped posters to every door,
they even stuck a poster
on the principal.

Andrew went home,
sure that his troubles
were over.

Chapter Three

When Andrew woke up the next
morning, he was very excited.
He ate, dressed and rushed
out the door.

But when he got to school,
there was only one pair of mittens
waiting for him, and they were
far too big.

Andrew put them in
his lunch box.

Just when he thought things
couldn't get any worse...

KNOCK! KNOCK!

Someone was at the classroom door.

It was Mr. Green, the principal.

"Whose posters are these?"
he grumbled, pointing to the one
that was still stuck on his back.

"They're mine,"
Andrew said quietly.

"Come with me,"
boomed the principal.

Chapter Four

Andrew could hear muffled sounds
coming from the office.
The principal opened the
door and hundreds of mittens
came pouring out
into the hallway.

Inside the office,
one secretary
was swinging from
the lights, and the
other secretary was
completely buried
in mittens — except
for the bun in her hair.

As they stood there
the pile grew...
out of the office...
down the hall...
and right into the classrooms.

"You have to do something,
Andrew!"
shouted the principal.

"Save us!"
screamed the secretary,
as she disappeared into
the sea of mittens.

Children and teachers
were being swept away
by thousands of mittens,
until finally the whole school
was filled.

Andrew quickly climbed out
a window and up onto the roof.
He ran along the top until
he was standing above
the front doors.

Reaching down,
he stretched his arm
as far as it could go.
And with the tip of one finger
he touched the top
of the door.

CRASH!

The doors flew open.

Out poured all of the students,
the teachers, the secretaries
and the mittens,
all mixed together to form
a magnificent mountain.
At the top of the mountain
of mittens, Andrew could see
Mr. Green's legs sticking out.

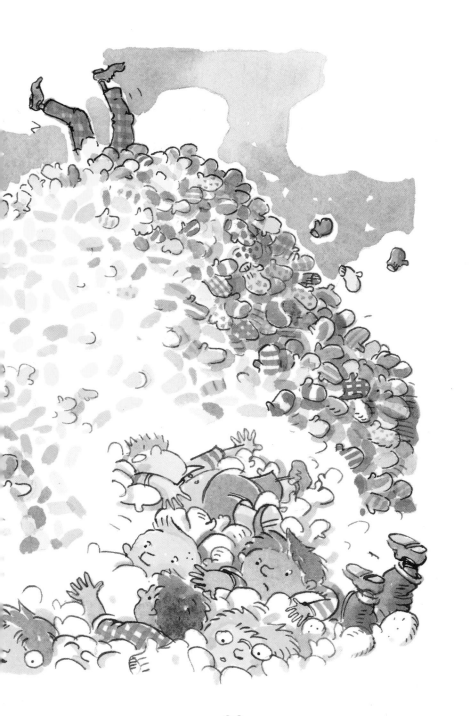

Chapter Five

Andrew ran inside the school
and called for help.

The firefighters, police and
ambulance came rushing
to the scene.

The police went to find the children's parents.

The firefighters used their tallest ladders to rescue the children.

And the ambulance stayed to make sure everyone was all right.

All of the children and teachers
were freed from the mittens,
but the firefighters
could not reach
Mr. Green.

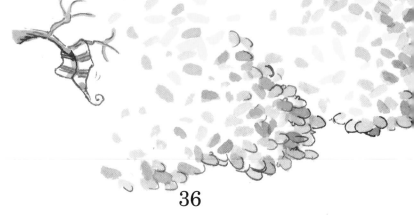

Andrew had an idea.
He borrowed a police officer's
bull horn and yelled for the
children to find their mittens.

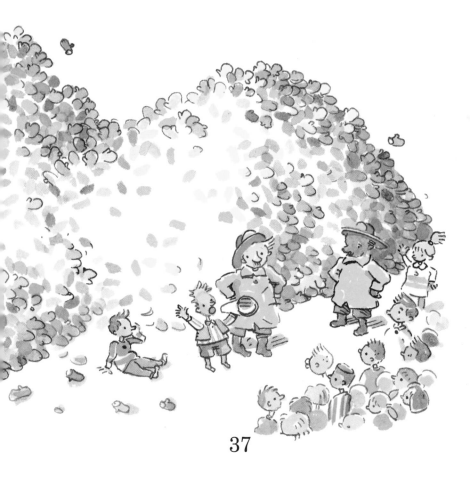

Everyone started looking.
At first it seemed impossible.
Then Ben shouted,
"Hey! Here's the blue one
I lost last month!"

One by one and faster and faster
the mittens were being claimed.

In one hour all of the mittens
had been sorted out,
Mr Green was safe, and
better still, Andrew had found
all of his missing mittens.

Chapter Six

Everyone was happy…everyone
except Mr. Green.
He walked up to Andrew
and sighed.
"I lost a pair of mittens,
and I was hoping that they
were here, but all of the mittens
have been taken," he said.

Andrew raced into the school
and came back with his lunchbox.

He opened it up and out
popped a large pair of mittens.
"My mittens!" cheered the principal.
He was so happy to find his mittens
he forgot all about what had
happened.

The parents were so pleased to have recovered their children's missing mittens that they quickly organized a parade with Andrew as Parade Master.

At school, Mr. Green presented
Andrew with a badge that said
LOST AND FOUND MONITOR.

Andrew rushed home to show the
badge to his mother and father.

He kicked off his boots,
tugged at his scarf,
unzipped his coat,
pulled off his mittens and
OH, NO!

Where was his hat?